KT-547-280

SAM WU

is <u>NOT</u> afraid of
GHOSTS

EGMONT

We bring stories to life

First published in Great Britain in 2018
by Egmont UK Limited
The Yellow Building, 1 Nicholas Road, London W11 4AN

ISBN 978 1 4052 8751 7

www.egmont.co.uk

A CIP catalogue record for this title is available from the British Library

67430/006

SAM WU

is NOT afraid of GHOSTS

See, totally NOT scared

KATIE & KEVIN TSANG

Illustrated by Nathan Reed

EGMONT

FOR OUR PARENTS

-Katie & Kevin Tsang

CONTENTS

CHAPTER 1

DON'T CALL ME SCAREDY-CAT SAM

My name is **Sam Wu** and I am <u>NOT</u> afraid of ghosts.

I know this for a fact because I recently had to become a genuine, certified[1] **ghost-hunter**. Some people might try to tell you otherwise. But those people are **LIARS**. Do <u>NOT</u> listen to them. Especially do not listen to them if their name is **Ralph Philip Zinkerman the Third**. Ralph will tell you

---

[1] Certification came from my friend Zoe but that's not important.

that I am . . . Scaredy-Cat Sam.

For the record, I am **<u>NOT</u>** a scaredy-cat.
If I were a cat, I'd be like my little sister
Lucy's cat, Butterbutt. **DO <u>NOT</u> BE
FOOLED BY THE NAME.**

Butterbutt is an

EVIL NINJA!

Even my Na-Na (that's my grandma — she lives with us) is **scared** of Butterbutt and she is so brave that one time **she wrestled an ALLIGATOR!**

When I tried to explain to Ralph that:

A. I am <u>**NOT**</u> a scaredy-cat and

B. Scaredy-Cat doesn't make sense as an insult

he just laughed at me and said I was probably scared of cats too. **Which obviously ISN'T TRUE.**

He's never met Butterbutt. I bet **he'd** be scared of Butterbutt.

I mean, seriously! LOOK AT HIM!

You are probably wondering why Ralph calls me **Scaredy-Cat Sam**.

Now listen closely, because I'm only going to tell this story **ONCE**. Okay? I don't even let my best friends Zoe and Bernard talk about it. And we talk about **everything**. But even they know <u>**NOT**</u> to ever mention it. It isn't a laughing matter, no matter what some people might tell you.

It should have been the **best day of the year**. It was the day of the class field trip to the **Space Museum**. It was all I had thought about for months. You see, the Space Museum had a **REAL** spaceship in it. The only spaceship I'd ever seen was on my favourite TV show

I was **so excited**, I even wore my special spaceman gear, which was carefully crafted by

6

SPACE BLASTERS' **number one fan** (i.e. me).

Unfortunately, space gear is expensive. So I had to be resourceful and make my own even better space equipment. All it took was a bike helmet, some cling film and a few flashlights (**it's dark in space**). I even made a custom SPACE BLASTERS shirt with some felt tip markers.

I thought it was going to be a **perfect day**.

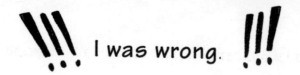 I was wrong.

It all started when I got on the bus to go to the museum. I sat down next to Zoe and Bernard, **proudly** wearing my SPACE BLASTERS T-shirt and specially crafted space helmet.

'Sam,' said Bernard, blinking at me. '**What exactly are you wearing?**' He was holding a lightsaber and wearing a Star Wars T-shirt. A fancy one. <u>**NOT**</u> one that he had made himself.

'Yeah,' said Zoe, frowning at my T-shirt. 'What's a space blaster?'

This was <u>**NOT**</u> the reaction I was expecting.

'Oh,' I said as I pointed at my T-shirt.

8

'This is Spaceman Jack and this is Captain Jane!' Or at least it was supposed to be. **Drawing is <u>NOT</u> one of my talents.**

My friends stared at me blankly.

'Spaceman Jack and Captain Jane?' said Bernard.

'Hmm . . . I should have drawn Five-Eyed Frank, huh? He's probably more recognisable.'

'Five-Eyed Frank? What are you talking about?' said Zoe.

I looked around the bus and I realised that **NOBODY** had any kind of **SPACE BLASTERS** gear on. I didn't get it! **SPACE BLASTERS** is the

BEST SHOW IN THE UNIVERSE. And BEYOND!

'You know — **SPACE BLASTERS?**'

Their expressions told me that they did **NOT** know about **SPACE BLASTERS.**

'It's all about Captain Jane and Spaceman Jack's adventures with their alien friend Five-Eyed Frank. They travel on TUBS, which stands for "The Universe's Best Spacecraft", and **BLAST** through wormholes to other galaxies and fight bad guys. It's the **BEST!**'

'So . . . it's like a less cool Star Wars?' said Bernard.

'No,' I scoffed. 'It's **WAY** cooler.' I actually wasn't totally sure. I'd never seen Star Wars.

Zoe and Bernard were still looking at me

like they didn't believe **SPACE BLASTERS** was the best show in all of the universe. 'You'll understand when you watch it,' I said.

'All right,' Zoe said, and Bernard nodded. And then we were at the Space Museum.

And that is when it all **REALLY** went wrong.

CHAPTER 2

THE UNFORTUNATE INCIDENT THAT WILL <u>NEVER</u> BE MENTIONED AGAIN

After waiting in a **super long queue** we were **FINALLY** in the Space Museum.

And it was **awesome**. We even got to go inside the spaceship! I felt like I really was Spaceman Jack.

'This is **AWESOME**,' I said.

Then someone snorted. That someone being the worst person in this galaxy, and maybe in all of the galaxies. That someone being Ralph Philip Zinkerman the Third.

'This place is so lame,' said Ralph. '**Real** space camp will be **way cooler**. I'm going inside an anti-gravity machine.'

If anything was going to ruin the trip to the space museum, it was Ralph. He'd told us all about how he was going to a fancy-schmancy space camp in the summer. The kind that costs **about a bajillion dollars**. The kind that I would give **ANYTHING** to go to.

'**Hey, Sam Wu-ser,**' said Ralph. He laughed an evil-villain laugh. He thinks it's **hilarious** that he could make my last name rhyme with loser.

For the record, this is TOTALLY <u>NOT</u> FUNNY!

14

Ralph knocked on my spaceman helmet. 'What is this thing on your head? Are you supposed to be an astronaut? I can't tell through all the lameness.'

'I'm **NOT** an astronaut,' I said. 'I'm a spaceman. **TOTALLY** different.'

Ralph snorted. Again. He's a master of snorts.

Before I could explain, Zoe jumped in.

'Sam is **OBVIOUSLY** Spaceman Jack,' she said. 'From **SPACE BLASTERS**. Haven't you ever heard of it?'

This is why Zoe is the **greatest friend in the history of the universe**.

'Spaceman Jack?' said Ralph, frowning. 'Sounds dumb.'

'Tell him all about Spaceman Jack and

15

Four-Eyed Fred!' said Bernard. He was bouncing next to me, waving his lightsaber around.

'Five-Eyed Frank,' I corrected, but it didn't matter. I looked Ralph straight in the eye. Just like Spaceman Jack always looks at the bad guys before he battles them.

'Spaceman Jack is the bravest being in all the galaxy.'

Ralph snorted (seriously he could win a snorting competition). 'And you are supposed to be this "Spaceman Jack"?' he said.

I nodded so hard that my helmet slipped over my eyes and I had to push it back up.

'Well, if you're **so** brave, why don't you get in _that_ thing?' Ralph smiled a nasty smile and pointed over my shoulder.

I slowly turned, then my **stomach dropped into my shoes**.

It looked like a **giant dinosaur egg**. If a giant dinosaur egg was also a bomb.

'It says **For Adult Riders Only**,' said a new voice.

It was Regina. Ralph's twin sister. But she **wasn't evil like he was**. 'Sam shouldn't go in that,' she said. 'And I think it's broken. It might be **dangerous**.' **!!!**

'I thought you were supposed to be some **brave spaceman?**' Ralph said to me. 'Or are you **too scared**, Sam Wu-ser?'

I swallowed and wiped some sweat from my eyebrow. 'I'm **NOT** too scared.' (I was pretty scared, but hiding it **incredibly** well, I thought).

'Come on, Sam!' Zoe whispered. 'Bernard and I will watch out for Ms Winkleworth. You can do it – show everyone that you aren't afraid!'

'**Don't do it, Sam!**' said Regina. 'You'll get in trouble. Or worse!'

By '**worse**' I think she meant that the Astro Blast Simulator could **kill me**. Because it looked like it could.

'Now, Sam! Ms Winkleworth is looking away – **this is your only chance!**' said Zoe.

'He won't do it,' said Ralph.

You can do it, Sam, said a voice in my head. It was the voice of Captain Jane, the captain of the Space Blasters crew. Sometimes, when I'm feeling **SLIGHTLY**

less brave, I hear Captain Jane or Spaceman Jack in my head. **Don't you think I was afraid when I went through my first wormhole? Or when I first saw the Ghost King on TUBS? Do it for the universe, Sam.**

I knew what I had to do. I couldn't let Captain Jane down.

I turned and looked at Zoe, Bernard and Regina. **I shot my hand up towards the sky like a rocket**. 'For the universe!' I declared and then, before I could change my mind, I ran as fast as I could towards The Astro Blast Simulator.

I hoped they didn't see how much I was shaking. **Which wasn't even that much**.

It was dark inside The Astro Blast Simulator. **Darker than I thought it would be**. Dark like in-space dark.

Before I even got my seat belt on or could turn on one of my flashlights, a countdown started.

'Five, four, three . . .'

'Wait!' I shouted at the Astro Blast Simulator. 'I **need to put my seat belt on!**' TUBS always listens to the Space Blasters when they yell at it.

The Astro Blast Simulator did <u>**NOT**</u> listen to me.

'Two . . . one . . . BLAST-OFF!'

And blast-off it did.

I finally understood what Spaceman Jack meant when he said blast-off felt like being **an egg scrambled in a hot frying pan**. The whole thing was shaking so hard I thought my head was going to fly off.

AND THEN IT STARTED SMOKING.

I coughed; **I couldn't breathe**; I bravely yelled for someone to make it stop, but it kept shaking!

And then I took matters into my own hands. I banged on the side of the walls. I kicked. I shouted, '**I command you to stop, Astro Blast Simulator!**' as loud as I could. But it didn't. **It was out of control!**

It was just like when Captain Jane's worst enemy, the Ghost King, took over TUBS. I tried to think what Spaceman Jack would do but all I could think was:

I'M GOING TO DIE.

And then:

OH NO, WHY DID I START THINKING ABOUT THE GHOST KING?

The Ghost King is the **scariest thing in the entire universe**. Even Captain Jane and Spaceman Jack are afraid of him. I like to think he's my **greatest fear** because I'm a **born spaceman**. And **ANYONE** with a brain would be afraid of the Ghost King.

100% **NOT** the time to think about the Ghost King!

And just when I thought it couldn't get worse, **THE FACE OF THE GHOST KING APPEARED IN THE SMOKE. HE WAS COMING TO GET ME.**

Goodbye, world . . .

And then there was light. The Ghost King must have got me. At least I died a brave death.

'Sam Wu! What <u>are</u> you doing?'

I blinked up into the light. The voice sounded angrier than a heavenly angel would. It actually sounded a lot like Ms Winkleworth.

'Sam! Get out of there, right now!'

I rubbed my eyes. It **WAS** Ms Winkleworth! **I wasn't dead!** I had survived, AND I had somehow defeated the Ghost King. And I was **<u>NOT</u>** afraid! I crawled out of the Astro Blast Simulator and **stood proudly in front of everyone.**

I was expecting applause.

I wasn't expecting what happened next.

A shocked silence.

Tumble
weed

And then . . .

HAHA HA HA! HA! HA HA HA!
HA HA! HA!
HA HA

Laughter. A lot of it.

HA HA HA! HA
HA HA! HA HA!

And rising above the laughter, Ralph's

voice . . .

'Sam Wu peed his pants!
Sam Wu peed his pants!
Scaredy-Cat Sam!
Scaredy-Cat Sam!'

I looked down.

It was true.

You should know that Spaceman Jack has **never**, ever peed his pants.

So. There it is. Don't ask me any questions about it. We'll never speak of it again.

But then I had to prove that **I WASN'T a scaredy-cat**. (And hope that I had banished the Ghost King for good.)

CHAPTER 3

BLAST-OFF ON TWO-WHEEL TUBS

After the **INCIDENT**, I knew I could never show my face at school again. Just like when Five-Eyed Frank got framed for an **evil crime** on his home planet and had to blast-off to a faraway moon.

As I'm sure you've gathered, unlike the **SPACE BLASTERS**, I don't fly spaceships so I didn't have the faraway moon option. Instead, I took off on my version of an intergalactic travel machine: **Two-Wheel TUBS**. (I named my bike after the SPACE BLASTERS' spaceship: TUBS, which stands for 'The Universe's Best Spaceship'. I added the 'Two-Wheel' so people would know it was a bike.)

I didn't know where I was going, but I just had to get out of town and escape the name 'Scaredy-Cat Sam'. I would have a **brave adventure**. And I would have to do it while Na-Na was napping and before my mum and dad got home from work.

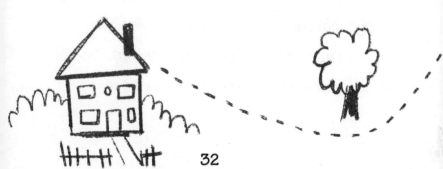

So I packed a bag with everything I'd need for my new life on the run:

- 🪐 My custom-made space helmet (to protect my head from ghost attacks)
- 🪐 My **extremely valuable** SPACE BLASTERS special edition collectible cards (for bartering)
- 🪐 Poison mist (my mum's hairspray)
- 🪐 Bag of rice (a spaceman's gotta eat)
- 🪐 Bottle of my favourite hot sauce (good for blinding ghosts and also for seasoning my food)

✧ Extra pair of underwear (just in case I had another ghost related incident)

I didn't want my family to worry, so I left them a note.

Dear Mum, Dad, Na-Na, Lucy and Butterbutt,

I'm very sorry, but the time has come for me to blast-off to the far beyond for a brave adventure, and to make a new name for myself. You'll probably never see me again. Don't believe any rumours you hear about me.

Mum, it was me who broke your favourite vase, not Butterbutt.

Dad, please stop doing the hokey-cokey at family parties.

Na-Na, sorry I won't be there to help you weed the garden.

Lucy, help Na-Na weed the garden. And don't let Butterbutt in my room.

Love,

Spaceman Sam

PS Watch out for the Ghost King. He's tricky – I know from experience.

It was almost a clean escape. But then my little sister Lucy came into the kitchen just as I was putting the rice in my backpack. She was holding Butterbutt **(who was looking especially evil)**.

'Sam,' she said, stroking Butterbutt, 'why are you putting a bag of rice in your backpack?'

'**None of your business!**' I said, without making eye contact with her.

She put down Butterbutt and started poking through my backpack. Butterbutt began attacking my ankles. I was definitely **<u>NOT</u>** going to miss him.

'What are you doing with Mum's hairspray?' said Lucy.

'That's **<u>NOT</u>** hairspray, it's poison mist

for me to use on my enemies. And put
it back.'

'You don't have any enemies,'
she said.

'I have plenty of enemies,' I said, grimly. But I didn't want her to be **too scared**, so I put on a tough voice and added, 'But that's nothing for you to worry about, little Lucy.'

Lucy frowned. 'Why do you sound so stuffy? Do you need to blow your nose?'

I glared at her. '**Never mind**,' I said. 'Now go back to your room. I've got things to do, places to go, **ghosts** to banish, things to **blast** . . .'

I swung my backpack on my shoulders with a grunt. It was heavier than I'd thought. It was probably the rice, which was taking up most of the space. I patted Lucy on the head.

'Be good for Mum and Dad,' I said. 'And help Na-Na in the garden.'

'**You're so weird**,' she said, but she went back to her room and Butterbutt followed her (with one final swipe at my feet).

And then it was time for my **great escape** – my **brave adventure**.

Yeah, definitely NOT going to miss him!

I couldn't even tell Zoe or Bernard where I was going.[2]

Unfortunately, it was still daytime, and I couldn't see the moon, so I stopped at the park and went on the swings for a while.

---

[2] I didn't really know where I was going. But I figured I'd just ride towards the moon and hope for the best.

I was pretty lonely, swinging by myself.
I was going to have to get used to that,
though, being **bravely** on the run, all alone.

I thought about when Spaceman Jack was
on the run from the Ghost King and what
he did. Then it hit me. **I needed a trusty
companion!** Just like Spaceman Jack had
his flying lizard, Three-Headed Tommy!

Three-Headed Tommy is **always** by
Spaceman Jack's side. Whether they're
eating on TUBS or getting sucked through
black holes or
exploring a
new galaxy,

wherever Spaceman Jack goes, Tommy is there too. So I knew I wouldn't get lonely (or only very occasionally a **tiny bit scared**) if I had my own trusty companion.

I hopped on Two-Wheel TUBS and sped to the pet shop.

CHAPTER 4

A DANGEROUS SIDEKICK

'What do you have?' I asked the pet shop owner.

'What is that thing on your head?' he asked, looking at my space helmet.

I glared at him. **That's <u>NOT</u> important.** I'm looking for something **fearsome** but **friendly**. Something I can take on an adventure. What do you have in stock?'

'What about a hamster? All the kids are

going nuts over hamsters these days.'

'**I don't want a HAMSTER**. I can't take a hamster on an adventure! Hamsters are scared of everything!' I lowered my voice. 'And they poop everywhere.' **The last thing I needed was a sidekick that pooped all the time.** 'I need something . . . tough.'

The pet shop man raised his eyebrows. 'Kid, all we've got here are rodents, small birds and reptiles. And they **all** poop.'

'Reptiles!' I didn't want to get my hopes up, but maybe he had something like Three-Headed Tommy! 'Like a . . . **a flying lizard?**'

The pet shop man scratched his head.

'Erm, no. In fact, we're fresh out of lizards, but I do have a snake you might be interested in.'

'A . . . a . . . snake? Like . . . a **real live** snake?'

'As real as they come. Hold on – I'll go and get it for you.'

Here's the thing. It's kind of a secret. **You can't tell anyone**. Especially **NOT** Ralph.

I'm a *little* bit scared of snakes.

But even Spaceman Jack is scared of snakes! They're terrible things to have on a spacecraft.

Or any flying device, for the record. **Or just anywhere**.

But before I could hop on Two-Wheel TUBS and zoom out of there at warp speed, the pet shop owner came back holding **A HUGE SNAKE**. Definitely **bigger** than any snake Spaceman Jack had ever seen.

'This is just a little guy and he's real sweet. Here, why don't you hold him?' He held the giant monster out to me.

There was **NO way** I was going to hold that snake. But I didn't want the pet shop owner to think I was a scaredy-cat. What if he somehow knew Ralph and told him? I considered my options.

'Oh, there's no need for me to hold it!'
I said, strolling over to the cash register. 'I
can tell that is a **high-quality snake**.
I'll take it.'

I whistled a little bit to show him just how relaxed I was.

'Great,' said the pet shop owner. And then he **PUT THE KILLER SNAKE AROUND HIS NECK** and went behind the till.

'Now, how are you going to pay for this guy?'

I reached into my backpack and got out my **SPACE BLASTERS** collectible cards. 'You're in luck. I've got some priceless **special edition collectible cards** I'm willing to part with,' I said.

The pet shop man laughed so hard

the snake nearly bounced off his
neck and on to the floor. **I took a small
step back**.

'Sorry, kid, I don't take trades. Cash or
credit only.' He pushed a phone towards
me. 'Why don't you call your
parents and ask them to
come on down? You should
ask them before you buy a
pet anyway.'

'**I can't call my parents**,' I said.

'Why not?'

I lowered my voice and looked from side
to side. Spaceman Jack always does that
when he says something secret. It was
hard because I didn't want to lose sight of
the snake, in case it made a sudden sneak

attack. Snakes are known for **being sneaky, after all**.

'Because I'm on the run.'

'Are you now?'

I nodded.

'What from? The law?'

'**Oh no, no, no!**' I didn't want him to call the police on me. 'Something happened . . . at school. And now **I can't go back.**'

'I see,' said the man, stroking the snake's head. I couldn't tell if the snake liked it or not. It only had one expression. **Ferocious**. 'Well, you know, having a snake might help you go back. There's no need to be on the run when you've got a tough sidekick with you.'

He had a point.

'And, I hate to break it to you, but I don't think you're going to be able to get very far with just your trading cards.'

I sighed. 'These are **NOT TRADING cards**. These are highly valuable special edition **SPACE BLASTERS** collectible cards.'

!!!

'Well, whatever they are, I don't want them. Now, here, go on and call your parents. Ask 'em to come on by and we'll sort everything out and get you home.'

How could he <u>NOT</u> want them?

Maybe the pet shop owner is right,
I thought.

Maybe I should go home.
Sometimes the **brave thing to do** is to
face your family and friends, **even if you
don't want to**. It would be kind of like when
Spaceman Jack had to go back to TUBS
after he **let the Ghost King get away**.

Plus, if I go back the owner of
**a dangerous snake, everyone
will see how <u>brave</u> I am.**[3]

---

[3] And I could own the snake without ever having to touch it.
Nobody would have to know.

But I couldn't call my parents, because (1) they were still at work, and (2) I knew what they would say.

Mum would say:

And if my mum said NO then my dad would say:

But Na-Na . . . Na-Na can be bribed. And if Na-Na said yes, well, she's my mum's mum so even my mum **has to listen to her**.

The pet store owner told me and Na-Na how to take care of it.

1. Put it in a glass enclosure with a secure but breathable lid. We got one with a sliding screen top.

2. Feed it a live mouse once a week. (Of course it **EATS ITS VICTIMS ALIVE**. At least it eats mice and not people. For now.)

3. Handle it regularly to get it used to human contact. **(NO WAY.)**

My mum and dad weren't thrilled about my new pet. But then Na-Na pointed out that it was **just the thing** to cheer me up after the **INCIDENT**. And she reminded my mum about the time she came home with a pet chicken when she was seven.

Na-Na: 1
Mum and Dad: 0

'You have to be responsible for it,' my dad said.

'Lucy's **NOT** responsible for Butterbutt!'

'Lucy is younger than you. And Butterbutt is the family pet. This snake is your very own. We trust you to take care of it,' he said.

'But don't you dare let any of those mice get loose,' **my mum said with a shudder**.

'It's okay if they get out! Butterbutt will catch them!' said Lucy. 'And I think the snake is cool!'

'It's not **COOL**. It's **DANGEROUS**,' I said. But I appreciated her support.

Lucy might be cool for a little sister, but she does <u>NOT</u> understand danger.

'Can I hold it?' she asked, coming up and knocking on the glass enclosure.

'**No!**' As well as bravely protecting Lucy from certain death, I also didn't want to let it out of the cage. '**It's extremely dangerous**. Not for children. Maybe when you are older.' **I gave my parents a knowing look.**

Then it was just me and my new sidekick.
Me and my snake. Him sitting in his
enclosure on top of my dresser. Me staring
at him, trying to show him who was boss. I
didn't blink.

He stared back. **He didn't blink either**.

I caved first. My eyes were starting to
water.

'I can't just keep calling you Snake,' I said.
'I've got to name you.'

He just stared at me. Then his tongue
flicked out. It was kind of creepy but at
least he was listening to me.

'What about . . . **Fang?**'
I was sure he had giant
fangs. Just like the snakes
on Planet Zoda. Sure, my

Fang

snake wasn't a snake from space, but all snakes had fangs, didn't they? Plus, Fang sounded scary. And tough. A scaredy-cat **DEFINITELY** wouldn't have a snake named Fang.

He stuck his tongue out again.

'Great,' I said, stepping away from the glass. 'Fang it is.'

Here's what I knew about Fang:

1. He didn't blink. **Ever**.
2. He ate things **bigger than his head**.
3. He was 'cold-blooded', whatever that meant. **Sounded dangerous**.
4. He wanted to eat me. **I was sure of it**.

Because of point 4, and because Fang is no ordinary snake, I put some of

Butterbutt's cat food in his tank to fill him up. Butterbutt wouldn't miss it.

Fang might have been my new sidekick, but I was watching him with **my eyes wide open**.

Except when I was sleeping.

Or blinking.

I should really learn how Fang never blinks.

CHAPTER 5

ALIEN CONTAMINATION

I might have gone back home, but I absolutely couldn't go back to school. There was no way. **Not a chance.**

This was obvious to everyone but my mum.

'Sam,' my mum said, 'I think you're just afraid of what that girl Regina is going to say.'

'Mum! I am **<u>NOT</u>** afraid,' I said.

I have no idea how she knows who Regina is. Or why she thought I would be afraid of

what she would say. My own mother might
as well have called me Scaredy-Cat Sam.
'I've been *contaminated!* **Probably by alien
germs**. Or worse . . . **ghost goop**. Who
knows? They even put up a sign around the
simulator that said contaminated.'

DANGER! BIO-HAZARD

My mum pinched the top of her nose and
sighed. She does that when she's getting a
headache.

'Sam,' she said. '**YOU were the
contamination**.'

'I was **NOT!**' I said, outraged.

'Fine. Not you. Your . . .' She gestured with her hands.

'Pee,' said Lucy proudly. 'I heard what happened. **You peed in the rocket.**'

'I did <u>**NOT**</u> pee in the **ROCKET**,' I said. I lowered my voice. 'One, it's called a **SPACESHIP**. Two . . . it was just in the simulator thing.' The last part came out as more of a whisper.

'We **aren't talking about pee any more** at the breakfast table,' said my mum. 'Now finish your congee.'[4]

'You still don't have proof that I don't have some kind of **alien disease**,' I said, poking my spoon in my congee. 'One time, on SPACE BLASTERS . . .'

'I don't care what happened on the space show,' my mum said. '**You're going to school.**'

---

[4] Congee is a rice porridge. It is my favourite thing to have for breakfast. Sometimes I even have two bowls. But sometimes I have pancakes. With chocolate chips. You can't put chocolate chips in congee.

For a minute, I wondered if my mum was working with the evil Ghost King. But that thought was **too terrifying** to consider. Even for someone **as brave as me**.

So I had to go to school. Zoe and Bernard stayed by my side, just like the SPACE BLASTERS stuck together during the hard times. Unfortunately, Ralph also stuck by my side. Like a **thorn** in my spacesuit.

'**Did you pee your pants again,** Scaredy-Cat Sam?' Ralph said when I walked past him.

I ignored him. That is what my dad told me to do when Ralph teases me.

Ignoring Ralph is <u>NOT</u> that easy!

I don't think my dad has any real life experience with this kind of thing, though.

And Ralph **wasn't** going to let anyone forget what happened at the Space Museum. I knew I was going to have to figure out a way to **prove to everyone** that I was <u>NOT</u> a scaredy-cat.

'Don't listen to him,' Zoe said at break-time, right after Ralph ran by shouting, '**Scaredy-Cat Sam! Scaredy-Cat Sam!**' for the tenth time that day. 'He's just being Ralph.' Easy for her to say. Ralph **never** bothers Zoe because she's the fastest, tallest person in our whole year.

Zoe

Sam's hair

Sam

Bernard

'Yeah, he's a just a jerk,' said Bernard. Bernard isn't taller or faster than anyone, but he is **one of the smartest kids** in our class.

And with Zoe being the fastest, and Bernard the smartest, I had to be the something-est, too. So I decided I'd be the bravest.

CHAPTER 6

DUCK, DUCK, TURNIP CAKE

Even Zoe and Bernard didn't believe that I was living with a **SUPER-DANGEROUS** predator.

'Aren't you . . .' Zoe lowered her voice, 'scared of snakes?'

'Zoe! You know we don't use the S word for Sam!' Bernard whispered.

'I am **<u>NOT</u>**—' I started to say.

'We know, we know. You **aren't** afraid,' Zoe interrupted.

'I'm **NOT**,' I grumbled.

'Well, can we come over and see it?'

'Yeah, Sam, can we come over? We've never been to your house.'

There was a reason for that. Multiple reasons.

1. **Butterbutt.** A total liability
2. Lucy. She'd ask **WAY** too many questions.
3. Na-Na. Her English isn't very good and I didn't want to **embarrass her.**[5]
4. We don't have any **normal** snacks at my house. My mum does her grocery shopping at the Asian supermarket.
5. Fang might eat **everyone**.

[5] I didn't want to be embarrassed either.

But they were right. How would anyone ever know about my **super-dangerous sidekick Fang** and how **brave** I was if nobody ever saw him?

'Okay,' I said. 'I'll ask my mum if you can come over tomorrow.'

I wanted to impress my friends, so I asked my dad to make my two favourite dishes. Roast duck, and turnip cake.[6] Usually he only makes them for **special occasions**, but I told him this **was** a special occasion. It was the first time I was having my friends over. And I was going to introduce them to SPACE BLASTERS! And it was the first time they were going to meet Fang. It would go

---

[6] A turnip cake isn't a cake like a birthday cake. It is a delicious square of fried turnips. In Cantonese it's called lo bak gou.

down in history as a **momentous occasion**.

When Zoe and Bernard walked through my front door, Bernard scrunched up his nose.

'**What's wrong?**' I asked. The last time I'd seen Bernard make that face was when he **accidentally** ate mouldy cheese.

'What **IS** that?' he said. His voice sounded all stuffed up, as if he was holding his breath.

'What's what?' I said.

Zoe held her nose. 'That smell! It smells like . . . **it smells like FEET!**'

I looked down at my feet and smelled as hard as I could. All I could smell was the delicious

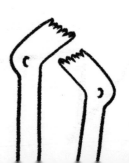

smells of roast duck and turnip cake. I guessed the turnip cake smell **WAS** kind of strong . . .

'Maybe you should put your shoes back on,' Bernard said.

'I can't,' I said. 'And um . . . you have to take your shoes off too. That's the rule at my house.'

'Maybe that's why everything smells like feet!' said Zoe.

Right at that moment, my dad walked out of the kitchen.

'Hi, kids! Hope you're excited for dinner! I made Sam's favourite!'

Just to be clear: my feet did **NOT** smell!

He held out the roast duck by the neck. 'Do you want to **help me chop it?**'

Bernard turned a little green. 'N-no thank you, Mr Wu,' he said.

Zoe's eyes looked like they were about to **pop out of her head**.

This was **<u>NOT</u>** going well. I had to distract my friends and I had to do it fast.

'Next time,' I said to my dad. 'I want to show Zoe and Bernard my room.' I turned to them. 'Come on, **let's go and meet Fang**. Unless you're too **scared** . . .'

Bernard eyed the duck warily. 'There is **no way it is going to be scarier** than **THAT**.'

CHAPTER 7

EVEN SPACEMAN JACK WOULD BE IMPRESSED

'**Meet Fang!**' I said, flipping on the light switch and proudly pointing at my dresser. 'The **toughest snake** there ever was!'

Zoe and Bernard crept in as if Fang might strike at any moment.

'Don't be **too scared**,' I said. 'He's just in his tank. He can't get out.'[7]

'Where is he?' Zoe asked.

---

[7] At least I hoped he couldn't get out.

'What are you talking about? **He's right there!**' I said, pointing at his tank.

'Right . . .'

My voice trailed off. I couldn't see him either.

'Sam,' said Bernard, 'is Fang an **imaginary snake?**'

'**Fang's real!**' I said. 'He's just . . . hiding.' I tapped on the glass, even though the pet store man had told me **NOT** to do that.

'**Why is he hiding?**' said Zoe, peering in the tank. 'I thought he was **tough**.'

'He **IS** tough. He's just . . . sleeping. Or something.'

'Or maybe he's going to **jump out** at you when you least expect it! **Like this!**'  a voice said from behind me, as small hands covered my eyes.

'ARGH!'

'**Gotcha!**' It was Lucy. She was cracking up. Even Bernard and Zoe were laughing.

'Lucy! Get out of my room!'

I said. 'I'm introducing my friends to Fang.'

Lucy stood on her tiptoes and looked in the tank. 'He's right **there!**' she said. 'Curled up behind the rock. He's playing **hide and seek!**' She pressed her nose against the glass and cooed, 'Hi, snakey-snake-snake!'

'Of course I knew where he was the whole time,'[8] I said, frowning at my sister. 'And stop baby-talking to my snake. He's tough!'

'That's Fang?' said Zoe. '**He's so tiny!**'

'He is **<u>NOT!</u>**' I exclaimed. 'He's just curled up. He's **TRICKING**

---

[8] I didn't.

80

you. He's incredibly **dangerous**. And **sneaky**.'

Just at that moment Fang decided to uncurl himself and **slither up the side of his tank**.

Zoe jumped back. '**Look!** He's trying to **get out!** Or maybe he's just trying to say hi?'

'See, I told you **he was sneaky**,' I said. 'And **dangerous**. You need to be very careful when you're around him.' I caught

Fang's eye and gave him a thumbs
up. He stuck his tongue out
at me. We were already making
a great team.

Bernard put his nose right
up against the glass. 'He's got a very
interesting pattern on his back,' he said.
'What kind of snake did you say he was?'

'The **most dangerous** kind,' I said. 'But
he's <u>**NOT**</u> poisonous.' I didn't want to scare
my friends **TOO** much.

Butterbutt bounded in and hopped on to
the dresser, headbutting Fang's tank. Fang
curled back up.

'**Lucy!** Get Butterbutt **out of
here**,' I said. 'He's being even more
annoying than usual.' I turned to my

friends. 'So . . . what do you think of Fang?'

'Definitely **a real snake**,' said Bernard.

'And definitely a **tough** one, despite his size,' said Zoe. 'I bet even Spaceman Jack and Captain Jane would be impressed with Fang.'

I beamed.

CHAPTER 8

LIGHTS OUT

At the dinner table, Bernard and Zoe were staring at their plates, **their mouths slightly open**.

'Where did your dad put the duck's head?' Bernard whispered to me.

'We don't eat the head!' I whispered back. 'Why would **anyone** do that?'

Bernard stared at me blankly. 'How would I know? **I don't want to eat it**. I just want to know where it went.'

'Sam, this **doesn't look like cake**,' Zoe whispered, poking her turnip cake with a chopstick. 'And **can I have a fork?**'

Dinner was <u>**NOT**</u> going well.

'Just try it,' I whispered back.

'This is Sam's **favourite meal**,' my mum said, smiling at us. She hadn't heard all the whispering. '**I hope you like it!**'

'I hope I like it too,' said Bernard. He didn't sound very optimistic. 'Any chance you also have chicken nuggets?'

'**Bernard!**' Zoe kicked Bernard under
the table. Then she looked up at my parents.
'**But do you?**'

I'd make a **huge** mistake. I should have
known better than to invite my friends over
to my house. What if they thought I was
Sam Wu-ser now, too? I looked down at my
delicious turnip cake.

'**How about I make you a deal?**'

my dad said, leaning forwards. 'If you try the duck and don't like it, **I'll order pizza**.'

'What about this thing?' said Zoe, poking her turnip cake again.

'**Let's just start with the duck,**' my dad said. 'I'll get you both forks.' '**You don't know how to use chopsticks?**' Lucy said, her eyes wide.

'Not everyone knows how to use chopsticks, Lucy!' I said. This was just getting **worse and worse**. At least I didn't need to worry about Na-Na saying anything embarrassing. She was tired so she'd already gone to bed.

Bernard and Zoe stared down at their plates.

'Maybe on the count of three?' I suggested. That always works on SPACE BLASTERS.

'All right,' said Bernard.

'Okay,' said Zoe.

'One,

   two,

       three!'

Zoe picked up the tiniest piece of duck with her fork and put it in her mouth. She chewed. And chewed. And . . .

Smiled!

'It's actually pretty delicious!' she said.

'Really?' I said.

'Really,' she said.

'Really,' said Bernard, taking another bite. And that made me **really**, **really happy**.

After dinner we went into the living room to watch a new episode of **SPACE BLASTERS**.

My mum even let us eat ice cream on the sofa. The evening had gone from a disaster to one of the **best nights ever**.

'Okay!' I said, bouncing on the couch. 'That's Captain Jane—'

'She looks **cool**,' Zoe interrupted.

'She is! And that's Five-Eyed Frank—'

'**He looks cool!**' Bernard butted in.

'Yes, he **is**! They are all cool. Now, like I said, their ship is called TUBS—'

'Like your bike?'

'Yes, like my bike. Now please listen so I can explain everything so you understand!'

I explained how on the last episode of SPACE BLASTERS the crew thought they had defeated the **Ghost King** but at the very end he came back. I told them the Ghost King was the **trickiest** and **most terrifying bad guy ever**.

The new episode opened with Captain Jane driving TUBS.

'**Spaceman Jack, do you hear that?**' said Captain Jane.

'**Hear what?**' said Spaceman Jack.

Captain Jane pointed above them. '**That sound. I've never heard it before.**'

'**Oh, it's probably just TUBS acting up again. Knock it off, TUBS,**' said Spaceman Jack as he elbowed the wall of the spacecraft.

'**That is not me,**' said TUBS in his robotic voice.

'**And it isn't me,**' said Five-Eyed Frank, his

mouth full of space worms and cheese.

'Chew with your mouth closed, Frank,' said Spaceman Jack.

Then all the lights went out on TUBS! (It was just like when I was in the Astro Blaster Simulator!)

'Oh no,' said Captain Jane. 'You know what that means.'

'The Ghost King is back!' said Five-Eyed Frank. His jaw dropped open and a few space worms climbed out.

Just then the TV sparked and

ALL THE LIGHTS IN THE HOUSE WENT OUT.

'Arghh!'

yelled Zoe.

'Arghh!'

yelled Bernard.

'MUM!'

I yelled.

My mum came running in.

'**Calm down** – we just blew a fuse. The

lights will be on in a few minutes,' she

said. 'Here, **I'll light some

candles**.' She put a candle on

the table and then left.

SCRATCH

The three of us sat around the candle. It flickered and cast shadows on the wall.

Then I heard it. **A scratching, clanking** sound. Right above our heads.

A sound very similar to one we had just heard on SPACE BLASTERS.

'Can you hear that?' I whispered.

CLANK

'Hear what?' Bernard whispered back. Bernard isn't great at whispering so it came out just as loud as his normal voice.

'Shh! I can't hear anything!' said Zoe.

The **scratching,**

SCRATCH

clanking sound
happened again.
This time it was **even
louder. And closer**.

'What is that . . .' Zoe said, but before
she could finish her sentence, THE CANDLE
WENT OUT. I knew what it was.

'It's the

GHOST KiNG!'

I said. '**He's back!**'

CHAPTER 9

WORMHOLES ARE REAL (AND GHOSTS ARE TOO)

'It's **<u>NOT</u>** a ghost,' said Zoe. '**Ghosts aren't real**. And the Ghost King definitely isn't real.'

Now that the candle had gone out, it was dark in the living room. **I could barely see** Zoe and Bernard.

'Weren't you watching that episode? This is exactly what happened to the SPACE BLASTERS!' I said.

'Sam, it looks like a cool show, but . . . **it's just a show**,' said Zoe. 'You know it isn't real, right? Just like ghosts aren't real?'

My face felt hot. I was glad my friends couldn't see me turning red. '**I KNOW** the show isn't real,' I said. '**But spaceships are real**. And worm holes. And moons. **And ghosts!**'

Bernard got out his glasses. He doesn't need glasses, but he likes to **wear them when he's thinking**. He says they make him **smarter**.

'There has been substantial research into ghosts,' he said. 'But we shouldn't jump to conclusions.' Bernard is **always**

saying things like that.

The noise happened again. This time it was even **louder** and sounded as if it was getting **really** close.

'Sam, are you sure it isn't just your house making weird noises?' said Bernard.

'Bernard, I've lived in this house my **WHOLE** life and it has **NEVER** made that kind of noise.'

It was true.

'And what do you think made the lights go out? And then the candle?' I added.

'I still don't think it's a ghost,' said Zoe but then, as if something was **ANSWERING** her, there was a

from inside the coat cupboard.

'What was that?' said Zoe, sitting straight up.

'It's **OBVIOUSLY** the **GHOST KING!**' I said. '**I told you!**'

'It is <u>**NOT!**</u>' said Zoe.

'Well if you are so sure it isn't, why don't you go and **look inside the cupboard?**' I said.

Zoe didn't move.

'That's what I thought,' I said, folding my arms across my chest.

'You . . . you really think there is a ghost in the cupboard?' said Zoe. She was **starting to sound scared**.

'Only one way to find out,' I said.

I took a deep breath. '**Let's open the cupboard**.' I couldn't believe how brave I was being. Probably **even braver** than Spaceman Jack would be in this situation. Just thinking about how brave I was being made **me a little nervous**.

See - totally <u>NOT</u> scared!

We crept up to the cupboard. My heart was beating so fast I was sure it was going to **jump out of my chest**.

'What are we going to do if we find the ghost?' said Bernard.

I hadn't thought that far.

'Zoe is super fast,' I said. 'She can catch it.'

'With what?' said Zoe. For someone who'd claimed she didn't believe in ghosts she **sounded pretty scared**.

'**With this!**' I said, grabbing a basket that my mum kept blankets in. I dumped the blankets out.

'I don't think we can catch a ghost with a basket,' said Zoe.

'This is all we've got! I don't have a

TURBO GHOST CATCHER 3000

like the **SPACE BLASTERS**, so this will have to do,' I said.

Zoe nodded. Bernard put his glasses back in his pocket.

'Okay,' I said, 'here we go!'

I took a deep
breath and pulled
open the coat
cupboard door. Then
something **FELL
ON US**.
  '**Arghhhh!**'
I yelled.
  '**Arghhhh!**'
yelled Bernard.
  '**I've got it!**'
yelled Zoe, throwing
the basket on me
and Bernard.
  '**Ow!** Zoe, that's
us, **<u>NOT</u>** the ghost!'
said Bernard.

The lights flickered – once, twice – and then came back on.

Bernard and I were sitting under a pile of **Na-Na's old sweaters**.

Bernard still had the basket on his head.

'So . . . no ghost?' said Zoe.

'But what knocked everything over?' said Bernard. 'The **ghost must have got away** before we could catch it!'

I was about to agree with him when we heard the **clanking sound** again. The sound that I'd **NEVER** heard before. 'And what is that sound?' I said.

Bernard's eyes were huge.

CLANK!

CLANK!

'Sam . . .' he said in a small voice, 'I don't think that is the Ghost King . . . **but I do think it might be a ghost.**'

'What do you mean?' Zoe whispered back.

Bernard leaned towards us. 'Haven't you ever seen *A Christmas Carol?* The ghost **ALWAYS shows up in chains!** That's why we're hearing chains. It all adds up! I think there might actually be **a ghost in the house.** But maybe **<u>NOT</u>** the Ghost King.'

'But the Ghost King might have **sent this ghost**,' I said. Bernard had made a good point, but as relieved as I was that it wasn't the Ghost King, I was sure that he was still involved. Somehow. He was tricksy like that.

'What are we going to do?' Zoe whispered.

'Let's go back to my room to make a plan,' I said.

'But . . . aren't you . . .' Zoe paused and exchanged a look with Bernard. I knew what that look meant.

'**I am <u>NOT</u> afraid!**' I declared. They didn't need to know how sweaty I was getting.

Back in my room, Bernard had gone into

research mode

and was on my computer looking up
everything he could find about ghosts. 'Okay,
okay. If there **really** is a ghost in the house,
our first step is to figure out what we want
to do with it,' he said.

'What do you mean, "**do with it**"?' I
asked.

'Do we want to **chase** it out of the
house? Do we want to **catch** it?'

'Catch it? What would we do
with it then?'

Bernard scrunched his
eyebrows together as he leaned
towards the computer.

'According to this website,
apparently we can **put it in a
bottle or something**.'

'A ghost **isn't** a genie!' I said.

'**Um, you guys . . . ?**' Zoe was staring at Fang's tank.

'And what would we do with it once it was in a bottle, anyway?' I went on. 'I think we want to chase it out of the house. Or . . . make it **evaporate or something**. Like on Ghostbusters.'

'You can't evaporate ghosts, Sam,' said Bernard in his **kind-of-annoying-I've-won-the-science-fair-three-years-in-a-row-so-I-know-everything voice**. Bernard is always an expert in everything. Even ghosts, apparently. But that's one of the

He holds the school record for science fair wins.

111

reasons I was glad he was on my side.

'You guys!'

Zoe shouted.

Bernard and I turned towards her at the same time. '**What?**'

She lifted a shaky hand and pointed at Fang's tank.

'**Fang's tank is open and he's GONE!**'

CHAPTER 10

THE MOST LOGICAL CONCLUSION

'Fang's <u>NOT</u> gone,' I said, trying to ignore the fact that my stomach felt like it was full of jumping beans. 'He's just hiding, like he was earlier. Snakes like to hide. **Right, Bernard?**'

Bernard came over and looked in the tank. 'I don't see him, Sam,' he said. 'Look **under** his rock!'

'**You** look under his rock!' I didn't want

to lift up the rock in case Fang was **actually** under it. He is, after all, **the most dangerous** pet snake in the galaxy.

'You just said you **didn't** see him!' said Bernard.

'YOU GUYS! THE TOP OF HIS TANK IS OPEN!' said Zoe. 'FANG IS DEFINITELY GONE!'

'Nobody would open Fang's tank . . . nobody except **THE GHOST**,' I said.

Zoe and Bernard gasped. Zoe **actually nearly fell over**.

Bernard nodded. 'That is the **most logical** conclusion. I **should** have thought of it myself.' Bernard is always disappointed when someone else figures out the answer to a problem before he does.

'What would a ghost want with a snake?' Zoe asked.

'Why do ghosts want anything?' said Bernard. 'To **SCARE** people! And what is scarier than a ghost? **A GHOST WITH A SNAKE**.'

Bernard was, once again, proving he is the brains of our group.

'So what are we going to do?' I said. I didn't know what I was more **worried** about:

1. The fact that my new snake was **loose**
2. The fact that **there was a ghost** in my house
3. The fact that the **ghost had let my snake out**
4. The fact that my **parents would find out** about my missing snake and ground me forever

I had promised, after all, to take care of Fang. And it was like my dad always says:

A Wu is only as good as their word.

Just then, my mum called out, '**Sam! It's getting late** – time to take everyone home!'

'You mean, what are **YOU** going to do. You heard your mum – we should probably be going,' said Bernard.

'**What?** You two can't leave me alone!' I said. '**There is a GIANT predator on the loose. And a GHOST**.' I didn't know the size of the ghost yet.

'**Five minutes, Sam!**' my mum called up.

'We'll be right down, Mrs Wu!' Zoe yelled back. 'Just . . . getting our stuff.' She came over and looked me in the eye. She had to crouch down a little to do it because she is **so much taller than me**.

'You'll be all right, Sam,' she said. 'And

we'll come back over to help you find the
ghost AND Fang.'

'But . . . what am I supposed to do
tonight?'

'Well,' said Bernard, 'I did just read that
pickles are apparently a **natural ghost
repellent.**'

'**Pickles?**' I said.

Bernard nodded wisely. 'Yes. I
just read it on this ghost website,
NaturalGhostRemedies.org. Some man
named Bob runs it and he sounds like a

ghost expert. If I were you, I'd **sleep in pickle juice.**'

'And maybe wear a protective suit,' said Zoe. 'You know, **just in case.**'

'Okay,' I said. 'That sounds . . .' It sounded **crazy** but I didn't have any better ideas. And if Bernard said it was a good idea, it probably was. Like I said, he's the **smartest kid I know.** 'All right. I'll do it.'

'Good luck tonight,' said Zoe solemnly.

I looked at them the way that Spaceman Jack looks at Captain Jane and Five-Eyed Frank right before he has to leave on a **secret mission.**

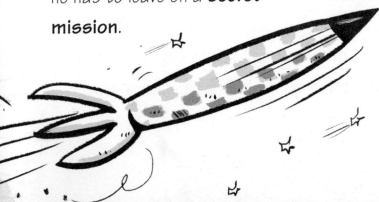

'If I don't make it through the night,' I said, 'I want you both to know that you are the **best friends in the whole world**. And you two can split my SPACE BLASTERS collectible cards.'

'Really?' said Zoe. '**Wow**, thanks, Sam. I know how much those mean to you.'

'Yeah, thanks, Sam. I call dibs on the **limited edition Five-Eyed Fred!**' said Bernard. 'He's my **favourite character** so far.'

I glared at them.

Zoe coughed. 'I mean, we hope you survive.'

'You'll be fine,' said Bernard. But then he hugged me, which he **NEVER** does. Zoe hugged me too. All the hugging was starting to **freak me out**.

'I'll **definitely** see you guys at school tomorrow,' I said in my bravest voice.

Zoe and Bernard **nodded nervously**.

'**Good luck**,' they said.

And then they left me. All alone.

CHAPTER 11

PICKLE CASSEROLE

After I brushed my teeth, I went into my parents' room.

'Mum? Dad?'

They looked at me. 'Sam, it's **past your bedtime** – what are you doing up?' said my mum.

I took a **deep breath**.

'I . . . I think there's a ghost in the house.'

My parents exchanged a look. A look that meant **they didn't believe me.**

I do **NOT** like this look.

'Sam, there's **NO** ghost in our house. **Ghosts aren't real**,' said my dad.

'But I've heard Na-Na talking about them!'

'Na-Na says a lot of things,' said my mum. 'You can't believe **all** her stories.'

'Why do you think there's a ghost?' said my dad.

I knew **I couldn't tell my parents** that Fang was **missing**. I'd only had him a few days. They'd never let me get another pet. It didn't matter that a ghost had let him out.

'I just heard something,' I said.

'You've been watching **too much of that space show**,' said my mum. 'Now **go to bed**.'

'But . . .'

'**Go to bed, Sam**.'

That was it. There would be no convincing them. It was going to be up to me,

I'm **NOT** a fan of this voice.

Zoe and Bernard to **catch the ghost**.

But tonight I was **on my own**.

And I had a **plan**.

I waited for everyone else to go to sleep, and then I **crept into the kitchen**, stealthily. Like when Butterbutt is stalking a butterfly.

I needed to get my supplies.

We only had **one pickle**, but all I needed was the juice. And some tinfoil.

I splashed some of the pickle juice on my face. No wonder this was a ghost repellent.

It smelled awful. Then I poured the rest of the pickle juice **all over my bed**.

Now it was time for my suit. This was where the tinfoil came in. First I wrapped my legs. Then my stomach. Then my arms. I even made a mask. I used the whole roll. The cardboard tube in the middle was an added bonus. It would make an excellent weapon.

Then I lay down. I was **extremely uncomfortable**. My sheets were **wet** and **smelled bad**, and the tinfoil was jagged and kept poking me in the back.

Also, I was starting to worry that maybe Bernard was wrong and ghosts didn't hate pickles but **LOVED** them. What if ghosts loved pickles? I'd basically turned myself into pickle casserole, ready to go into the oven. **A perfect dinner for a ghost.**

pickle →

'Okay,' I said to myself, 'stay calm. Stay calm. **What would Spaceman Jack say?**' I looked up at my Space Blasters poster. **These are the times that separate the brave from the scaredy-cats**, I imagined him

saying to me. **Don't be afraid, Spaceman Sam.**
You're gonna be just fine.

And I was **<u>NOT</u>** afraid.[9]

I DID <u>NOT</u> SMELL GOOD!

---

[9] I was very afraid. And I smelled very bad.

CHAPTER 12

ALWAYS BLAME BUTTERBUTT

I woke up soggy and pickled. I had survived the night, **but just barely**. I was **SURE** I heard the ghost at least **forty-nine times** throughout the night. But my pickle juice repellent must have worked.

'Sam! **You stink!** And what is all over your sheets? Did you have a nightmare and **wet the bed again?**' my mum asked at breakfast. 'Is this about the ghost?'

'I did **NOT** wet the bed,' I said.

'I just . . . **spilled**.' Butterbutt came up and licked my leg. Then he **licked it again**. I think he was tasting me. Pickle juice might repel ghosts but cats seem to like it.

'Spilled what?' my mum said, wrinkling her nose.

'**None of your business**,' I said. I picked up a newspaper and pretended to read it. That's what my dad always does when my mum asks him a question he doesn't want to answer.

This *always works* for Dad.

I didn't even get to the end of the first headline when my mum ripped the newspaper out of my hands.

'**WU GABO!** It most certainly is my business,' she said. '**Tell me what you did**. I know that **guilty face**.'

Uh-oh. She was using my **Chinese name**. Not only was it her business, but **she meant business**.

'I spilled . . . pickle juice,' I said, as if it were the most normal thing in the world to spill all over your bed.

My mum sighed and closed her eyes. 'And why did you have a jar of pickles in your room in the **middle of the night?**'

'**It's my fault**,' said Lucy.

'What?' my mum and I said at the same time.

Lucy nodded and opened her eyes really wide. 'I'm sorry, Mum,' she said.

'I was trying to open the pickle jar and I couldn't so **I asked Sam to open it for me.**'

'You don't even like pickles,' my mum said, looking back and forth between us. I didn't know what Lucy's plan was, but I trusted her. **We are always on the same team.**

'But Butterbutt **loves** pickles,' said Lucy. 'He wanted a midnight snack.' Sometimes Lucy thinks she can read Butterbutt's mind. 'So I asked Sam to open the jar. And when he was opening it, **Butterbutt jumped on him** and the pickle juice spilled everywhere.'

A classic Lucy move. **Blame Butterbutt**. Butterbutt is easily blamed. Plus, most things **really are** Butterbutt's fault.

Butterbutt can be useful to have around, sometimes.

My mum frowned. 'That's . . . strange,' she said. 'Anyway, whatever happened, Sam stinks. **Go hop in the shower right now**. And be quick or you'll be late for school.'

Sometimes, Lucy can be a pretty good little sister.

CHAPTER 13

GHOST-HUNTERS AND SNAKE WRANGLERS

During break, Zoe, Bernard and I met in our spot by the fence.

'**You survived!**' said Zoe. She gave me a high five.

'I guess this means we **don't** get your SPACE BLASTERS cards,' said Bernard.

'If you guys help me find Fang and get the

ghost, I'll think about giving each of you one of my **special edition cards**,' I said.

'Really?' said Zoe.

'Really,' I said. 'Because I'm going to need your help. **This is serious business**.'

'That's okay,' said Zoe. 'You don't need to give us your cards. We'll help you anyway. Right, Bernard?'

Bernard looked at his shoes. 'Umm . . .'

'**Right, Bernard?**' said Zoe again.

'Right,' he said. 'Friendship first. You can't bribe a good man.' He **grinned** at me. 'I heard Spaceman Jack say that on the show last night.'

'**I don't want to scare you**,' I said, 'but you should probably know what we're up against.' I lowered my voice. 'I heard the ghost **ALL NIGHT**.'

'What did it sound like?' said Zoe.

'You know how the washing machine sounds? All rattly?'

They nodded.

'Like that. **But louder!** And I heard whistles! Like a train! Is there a train anywhere nearby?'

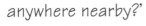

'I don't know,' said Zoe. 'Is there?'

I spread my arms out wide. '**Do you see any trains?**'

'Good point,' said Bernard. 'I'm impressed by your logical deduction.'

Just then, a football soared through the air and **hit Bernard** on the back of the head.

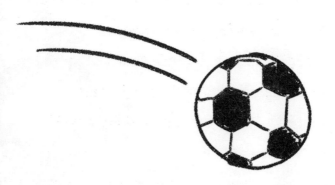

'**Ow!**'

Ralph came running over. Wearing his bow tie, **like always**. I once heard him say he thought it made him look 'sophisticated'.

I'm <u>NOT</u> sure it does.

'What are you losers talking about?' he said with **a sneer**.

Zoe took the ball and kicked it over the fence. '**Whoops!**' she said. Zoe is great to have around in moments like these.

'We're <u>**NOT**</u> losers,' said Bernard, brushing grass off the back of his head. 'As a matter of fact,' he took a deep breath, 'we're **ghost-hunters**.'

'Yeah,' I said, standing next to him. 'We're ghost-hunters. **AND** snake wranglers.'

Ralph took a small step back. 'G-ghosts?'

he said. 'What ghosts?'

'There's one in Sam's house!' said Zoe. 'And we're going to get it.'

'We're **NOT scared of ghosts**,' I said.

'Really?' Regina had walked up behind Ralph. 'Because Ralph and I think there is a ghost haunting **OUR** house!'

'It's **NOT** a ghost, Regina,' said Ralph. 'It's a **zombie werewolf!**'

Regina turned to me. 'We don't know what it is.

But there is definitely **SOMETHING** in our basement. Ralph won't even go down there any more.'

Ralph scowled at his sister. '**Be quiet**, Regina!'

Regina ignored him. This made me **happy**. 'Are you **really** a ghost-hunter?' she asked me.

I nodded and **puffed out my chest**. 'We're probably the **best ghost-hunters in town**.'

'I **don't** believe you.' said Ralph.

'If we catch our own ghost then we'll come to your house and help you catch your ghost.'

I made my voice sound **extra-brave**.

'Ralph's right, though,' said Regina. 'It might be something worse than a ghost. Something **scarier**.'

'Yeah, and we know what happens to **Scaredy-Cat Sam** when he gets scared,' said Ralph with a signature snort.

'Whatever is in your basement, I **won't** be scared of it!' I declared. This was my chance to prove that I wasn't Scaredy-Cat Sam. My chance to prove I was even **braver than Ralph**.

'You haven't even caught your own ghost yet,' said Ralph. 'Or your **imaginary** snake.'

'Fang is <u>**NOT**</u> imaginary!' I said. 'We'll find Fang and we'll catch our ghost, and then . . .'

I pointed to the sky in the **SPACE BLASTERS** stance, 'we'll be ready for anything!'

Zoe and Bernard did the same move.

'For the universe!'

they declared. For seeing just one episode of **SPACE BLASTERS**, they sure had caught on fast.

CHAPTER 14

THINK LIKE A GHOST

Zoe and Bernard came over on Saturday to help me catch the ghost and find Fang.

'I did some more research on ghosts last night,' said Bernard, putting on his **thinking glasses**.

Zoe and I looked at him expectantly.

'There are **five different types of ghost**.

And they are . . .

Hungry ghost,

angry ghost,

pesky ghost,

haunting ghost and

lost ghost.'

152

None of those sounded very nice. 'What about a **friendly ghost**?' I said. 'Maybe there are six types of ghosts.'

Bernard shook his head. '**Nope**,' he said. 'Only the five. But the good news is, I think our ghost is **a pesky ghost**. And that's the best and least scary one to have.'

'I still think a friendly ghost would be better,' I muttered.

'How do you know it is a pesky ghost?' asked Zoe.

Bernard blinked. He **doesn't** like it when anyone questions him. 'It's **simple**,' he said. 'It let the snake out as a prank. Only a pesky ghost would do that.'

'I thought you said it did that to be **scary**,' I said.

'It can be pesky **and** scary at the same time,' said Bernard.

I nodded. That **did** make sense.

I was glad to have Bernard on our ghost-hunting team.

'So how do we get rid of a pesky ghost?' said Zoe.

'**Ah**,' said Bernard. 'That's the **tricky part**. We're going to have to **think** like a pesky ghost.'

That is how we ended up sitting around wearing sheets on our heads with eye holes cut out of them.

'I **don't** feel like a pesky ghost,' said Zoe.

'I just **feel stupid**.'

'Then you aren't trying hard enough,' said
Bernard.

'We haven't **seen** our ghost,' Zoe
went on. 'How do we know they even
look like this?'

'**Eureka!**' I shouted, standing up so
fast my sheet fell off. Eureka is what

Spaceman Jack says when he has a **really brilliant idea**. 'We have to **SEE** the ghost to get rid of it!'

'How are we going to do that?' said Bernard.

'I've got a plan,' I said, smiling at my friends reassuringly. '**Follow me**.'

Luckily, my parents were at Lucy's karate competition and Na-Na was napping, so we had the house to ourselves. I led my friends into the kitchen.

Kitchen, this way

'Why are we in the kitchen? I've already established that our ghost isn't a **hungry ghost**,' said Bernard.

'Our biggest problem is that the ghost is **invisible**,' I said, pulling over a chair to stand on.

'No, our **biggest problem** is that there is a ghost **and** a snake on the **loose in your house**,' said Zoe.

'Hold my chair steady,' I said. I bravely climbed on to it so I could reach the top shelf where my mum kept all the baking things.

'If we can **SEE** the ghost, we'll be able to chase it away!' I said.

'But we can't see the ghost,' said Zoe, sounding **annoyed**. 'And even if we could see it, wouldn't we still be scared of it?'

'Zoe, you're the fastest girl in our year—'

'Fastest **person**,' she interrupted me.

'**Exactly!** You'll be great at chasing the ghost.'

'Or running **away** from it,' said Bernard.

'Either way, you'll be fine,' I said. 'Here, take this.' I passed down a bag of flour.

'But what about us?' said Bernard. 'If Zoe is running away from it . . .'

'**Chasing it**,' I corrected, as I grabbed a bottle of honey.

'Then what are we doing?'

I hopped down from the chair. 'Let me tell you my **master plan**.'

Once I explained my whole master plan to Zoe and Bernard, they were much more **impressed**. We just had to put it in action.

Turn over for
SAM WU'S
MASTER
PLAN!
(You will **NOT**
be disappointed)

MASTERPLAN

☐ **Step 1:** Open **all** the windows (to let the ghost out)

☐ **Step 2:** Set **flour traps** on top of the kitchen door (to coat the ghost so we could see it)

☐ **Step 3:** Pour honey on the floor to attract the ghost. (**Everything** likes honey, even ghosts. I know this because that was how the **SPACE BLASTERS** once caught the Ghost King on TUBS.)

☐ **Step 4:** Bring **fan** into the kitchen

☐ **Step 5:** When the ghost triggers the flour trap, chase ghost with fan to **blow it away**

After we'd completed steps 1–4, Bernard **scratched his head**. 'One question, Sam. Once we blow the ghost out of the house, how will we find Fang?'

'We'll go into that **wormhole** when we get to it,' I said. This is another one of Spaceman Jack's sayings. 'Let's all get under the kitchen table so we can take the ghost by **surprise**.'

After half an hour, the ghost still hadn't come. We hadn't even heard it all morning.

'Are you sure this is a pesky ghost?' Zoe said with a yawn. 'I think it's a **BORING** ghost.'

'**Shh!** Don't insult it,' said Bernard. 'That will just make it an **angry ghost!**'

'Wait,' I said. 'Maybe Zoe is on to something! Maybe we can lure it by **mocking it.**' I took a deep breath. **'You're a silly ghost!** A scaredy-cat ghost! I'm <u>NOT</u> afraid of you at all!'

I shouted as loud as I could.

We paused.

. . .

. . .

. . .

And then we heard it. A **creaking**; a **groaning**. Something coming closer . . .

'It's working!' Zoe said. 'Keep going!'

'You're a . . . **smelly ghost!** A not very scary ghost!'

The creaking was getting **louder** . . .

CRREEEAK!

'What if the fan doesn't work? What do we do?' said Bernard.

'We **definitely** need to protect ourselves,' said Zoe. 'Here, grab these pans just in case.' Zoe handed **a wok** to Bernard and a large pot to me.

I **immediately** put the pot on my head.

'You're the worst ghost ever! **Come and get us!**' I yelled.

There was a long pause. Suddenly, a gust of wind tore through the room and the kitchen door started to creak open.

'It's **HERE!** The ghost is here!' yelled Bernard. '**Turn on the fan!**'

'The fan won't turn on! We **forgot** to plug it in!' said Zoe.

Spaceman Jack always takes charge in times like these.

'Both of you **stay back!** Let me take care of this!' I yelled.

Without a real plan, I jumped up from under the table and ran at the opening door, **waving my arms** like a windmill.

'AHHHHH! GO AWAY, YOU PESKY GHOST! I'M COMING FOR YOU!'

I yelled. But as I ran, the pot fell **over my eyes**. It was too late to stop, so I kept on towards the door with my arms still swinging like **blades**. As fast as I could. **Straight at the ghost.**

'Sam! **Wait!**' I heard Zoe shout from behind me.

I smashed straight **into the ghost**. It was surprisingly solid for something that was **invisible**. We toppled over into the honey on the floor.

'**OW!**' I heard. The voice was **familiar**. I got a **sinking feeling** in the pit of my stomach.

'**SAM! What is going on?**' said the ghost. Except it **wasn't** the ghost . . .

I took the pot off my head. I was lying on top of **Na-Na** . . . who was covered in **flour**. And **honey**. She did **NOT** look very happy.

She actually looked even **scarier** than a real ghost. **Even the Ghost King.**

'Sam! Who is that? That's **<u>NOT</u>** the ghost!' said Bernard.

'Nope,' I said, as I stood up and held out a hand to help Na-Na up. 'This is my grandma, Na-Na. Na-Na, these are my friends, Bernard and Zoe.'

'**And you are all in very big trouble**,' said Na-Na.

CHAPTER 15

A SHOCKING REVELATION

Our first ghost hunt had been a **complete disaster**. Not only did we <u>**NOT**</u> catch the ghost, we had to spend the whole afternoon cleaning the kitchen. And after that Na-Na made us **weed the garden** for HOURS. And she said that ghosts definitely **were** real but this was <u>**NOT**</u> the way to catch them. Then she went back to her nap.

'I can't tell if your grandma is **really brave** or **really sleepy**,' said Zoe.

'Or just really **cranky**,' added Bernard.

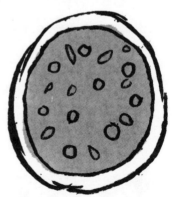

Na-Na might even be braver than me.

'All three,' I said.

The ghost was still on the loose. And Fang was still lost. And getting hungrier by the minute.

The day got a little better when my parents came home. They brought us **pizza for dinner**. And Na-Na didn't even tattle on us. She just made a mark in her diary and I knew that **I owed her forever**.

I am going to be weeding the garden for the rest of my life.

After dinner, we went into my room.

'We have to come up with a **new plan**,' I said.

Zoe yawned. 'Can we watch another episode of the **SPACE BLASTERS** instead? I'm getting bored of chasing the ghost.'

'Easy for you to say,' I said. 'You don't have to sleep here **every night**, wrapped up like a pickle casserole, wondering if the ghost is coming for you!'

'**Or the snake**,' said Bernard. He'd put his thinking glasses back on.

'Fine, fine,' said Zoe. 'We'll help you catch the ghost. But I'm **never** helping you weed the garden **ever again!**'

The door started moving and we all froze.
Maybe it was **the ghost!**

It was Lucy. She was still in her
karate uniform.

'I want to help catch the ghost,' she said.

'**Go away,** Lucy! We're having a very
important meeting,' I said. 'You're **too
little** to help catch the ghost.'

'**Wait!**' said Bernard. He narrowed his
eyes at Lucy. 'How do you know about the
ghost? We never told **you** about it. Are you
working with the ghost?'

Lucy rolled her eyes. 'I thought you were
Sam's smart friend,' she said.
She pointed at the vent in the
corner of my room.

'That connects to my room,' she said. 'I can hear **everything**. You guys are pretty **loud**. Especially Bernard.'

'Well, it doesn't matter how you know,' I said. 'You can't help us. **I'm sorry**. We have to protect you from the ghost.'

Lucy stamped her foot. 'But I'm <u>**NOT**</u> afraid of the ghost!'

Here's a secret about Lucy. She actually isn't afraid of **ANYTHING**. I've seen her catch spiders and jump off the highest diving board at the pool. And she's the only one in the family who Butterbutt listens to. Even Butterbutt knows **not to mess with Lucy**.

'Sam, we do need help,' said Zoe. 'We're all out of ideas.'

I frowned. I was supposed to be leading this ghost hunt. Not my little sister. But Zoe had a point.

'Okay, fine,' I said. 'You **can** help.'

'Hooray!' said Lucy. 'Can we have a cool

name? Like a team?'

'This **isn't** a game, Lucy!' I said. 'This is **very serious business**. This isn't pretend. **It's dangerous**. We're really going to catch a ghost, and I need you to be . . .'

But Lucy wasn't listening. Her eyes grew wide as she went over to the wall and put her ear against it.

'Shh! Listen!'

she said.

We all went **very quiet**.

There it was! The ghost! I could hear it **scratching** and **clanking**.

'It's **IN** the wall!' Bernard said, his ear pressed to the wall now too.

This was it. Time to get the ghost.

'The sound is getting quieter. The ghost must be **escaping!**' said Zoe.

'It sounds like . . . it's going . . . in **that direction!**' said Bernard, pointing to the corner of my room. 'What is on the other side of that wall?'

'**My room!**' said Lucy. We all ran into her bedroom. I **didn't have a plan** but I couldn't let the ghost get away. A plan always comes to the SPACE BLASTERS at the very last minute. It would be the same for us.

There were **dolls** and **toy cars** and **crayons** all over Lucy's floor. Bernard tripped on a car and fell.

'**The ghost tripped me!**' he yelled.

'No, you just tripped over a toy,' said Zoe, pulling him up.

'Is the ghost in here?' said Lucy. 'I don't see it.'

'**Here!** I've been saving this just in case!' said Zoe. She reached into her pocket, pulled out a sandwich bag filled with flour from earlier and threw it into the air. **Clouds of white floated** all around us and landed on the floor. And in our hair.

'**No ghost**,' said Bernard, wiping flour off his glasses.

But the sound was getting **louder**.

'It's getting **closer!**' I said. 'I think it's **IN** the wall!'

'How are we going to get inside the wall?' Zoe moaned.

'**Like this!**' said Lucy, and she went to the vent in her wall and pulled the cover off.

'Whoa!' said Bernard. 'When did Lucy get **super strength?**'

Lucy grinned. 'This is my **secret space!** I took out the screws forever ago. I hide all my money in here. I had to stop using my piggy bank because Mum kept going into it when she needed change.'

'**What money?**' I asked. How did Lucy have any money to hide?

'Christmas, birthday, tooth fairy money

and whatever Mum leaves on the kitchen counter,' she said, counting it all off on her fingers.

'This is **<u>NOT</u>** the time to be thinking about finances,' said Bernard.

Lucy peered into the vent. 'Yep, the ghost has definitely been in here! **And he's knocked over all my coin towers!**'

We all scrunched next to Lucy to look inside. The opening was **small and square** — the same shape as a shoebox. It was dark in the vent, but we could still see into it.

And **Lucy was right**, her coins had all been knocked over.

Then we heard it again. The **clanking** sound. It **was** the ghost! And it was coming towards us!

CLANK

'I SEE ITS EYES!'

Bernard yelled.

'I SEE THE GHOST'S EYES!'

'That's **NOT** the ghost,' I said. I knew
what we were up against now. I recognised
those beady eyes. **'It's Fang.'**

Zoe screamed. 'That's even scarier!
FANG IS GOING TO EAT US.'
**'THE GHOST WANTS FANG
TO EAT US!'** shrieked Bernard.

'I WAS WRONG! It's **NOT** a pesky ghost! It's an **ANGRY GHOST. AN ANGRY GHOST AND A HUNGRY SNAKE.** The worst possible combination!'

Now that we were facing both Fang **AND** the ghost, I didn't know what to do. I was really glad Ralph and Regina weren't there to witness how **NOT** brave we were being. Although the others seemed to be getting a bit **out of control**, if you asked me. We needed to work together.

'It's **only** Fang!' Lucy said. 'You just have to get him out.'

'I'm **NOT** getting him!' said Zoe. 'What if he bites me?'

'He **won't** bite you,' said Lucy. 'He's a boa. Mum said boas **don't have fangs**.'

'His name is *Fang*,' said Zoe. 'He'll **definitely** bite me.'

Bernard scratched his head. 'Lucy's right, though — I don't think he has actual fangs. I looked it up. He's misnamed.'

'Who cares what his name is?' said Lucy. 'We've got to **get him out. Look!** He's already getting away!' As he slid away over the coins, we heard the scratchy ghost sound again. And then he knocked into another pile of coins, making the **clanky ghost sound**.

'The ghost sound! **It's just Fang** on the coins!' I said, but nobody heard me.

'**Get him, Sam!** He's **your** snake!' shouted Zoe.

Here it was. My chance to prove, once and for all, how **brave** I was. I took a deep breath. I was going to do it.

On the count of one, two . . .

'**I've got him!**' said Lucy, triumphantly yanking Fang back by the tail.

'I would have got him,' I muttered, but Lucy was already carrying him back into my room.

185

We all ran after her.

She put Fang in his tank and slammed it shut. '**There!**'

'But what about the ghost?' said Zoe.

I took a deep breath and looked at my friends. I was going to make a **shocking revelation**.

'I don't think there is a ghost.'

CHAPTER 16

BUTTERBUTT STRIKES AGAIN

'**No ghost?**' said Zoe. 'But . . . we heard it!'

I shook my head. 'We heard **Fang** on the coins. That was what was making the **scratching noise**, and the **clanking**.'

'But what about the whistling? And the cupboard? And the **lights going out?**'

I didn't have an answer to that. 'I don't know,' I said. 'Some **mysteries** aren't meant to be solved.' That's what Captain

Jane says whenever Spaceman
Jack asks her a question
about the universe she
doesn't know the
answer to.

'And,' said Bernard,
'who let Fang out?'

'I don't know,' I said again, putting my face
in my hands. Not only was I **NOT** a ghost-
hunter, or a snake-wrangler, but I was an
awful detective. The **SPACE BLASTERS** would
be so **disappointed in me**.

'Maybe the ghost let Fang out and then
left,' suggested Zoe.

'Maybe,' I said. 'But **if** there is a ghost
in the house, I don't know how we'll ever
catch it. **Na-Na was right** – we don't

*And I did **NOT** know the answer.*

know what we're doing.'

Just then the door **creaked open**. But nobody appeared! Bernard gasped and Zoe covered her eyes. **I kept mine open**. I wasn't going to miss the ghost again.

Butterbutt sauntered in and pounced on me.

'Ugh,' I said, pushing him off. 'It's just Butterbutt. Get out of here, you **evil cat**.'

But Butterbutt wasn't listening to me.

He had his hunting face on. He **crouched down low,** his eyes alight.

'Maybe Butterbutt sees the ghost!' said Lucy. **'Can't cats see ghosts?'**

Without warning, Butterbutt leaped up into the air and landed on my dresser.

We all watched as he went up to Fang's tank and

PULLED THE LID OPEN with his paws!

'Butterbutt **is** the ghost!' I said.

'I can't decide if that's the **smartest cat** I've ever seen, or the **stupidest**,' said Bernard.

Lucy stepped forwards and scooped up Butterbutt. '**Bad kitty!**' she said. She turned to me. 'You should get a lock for the top of that.'

'You should watch **your** cat,' I muttered. But she was right – Fang was already trying to slither up the side of the glass enclosure and escape . . . **again!**

'<u>**NOT**</u> today, buddy,' I said, closing the lid, careful **<u>NOT</u>** to touch Fang.

Although I had to admit, after all of this, Fang didn't seem **so scary any more**.

CHAPTER 17

CERTIFIED GHOST-HUNTERS

'So what happened to your ghost?'

Zoe, Bernard and I were minding our own business in our spot on the playground when Ralph **swaggered over**. Wearing his bow tie, of course.

'**Why do you care?**' said Bernard.

Ralph shrugged. 'I don't believe you. I don't

believe you had a ghost **or** a snake in your house.'

'We chased the ghost out of the house,' said Zoe. (We'd decided that was our **official story** and we were sticking to it.) 'We're certified ghost-hunters now. We've even got **these**.' She handed him our official ghost-hunter certificates.

She was the one who made them, but Ralph **didn't** need to know that.

'What matters is that we were prepared,' she said when she gave them to us. 'And if there **HAD** been a ghost, we would have been **ready for it**.'

'Would we have?' Bernard had asked, looking **sceptically at the ghost-hunter certificate**.

'Definitely,' said Zoe. She'd even made a certificate for Lucy, who had hung it up on her wall **next to her karate trophies**.

Ralph frowned at the certificates. 'This doesn't prove **anything**,' he said. 'I still think Sam Wu-ser is a **big scaredy-cat baby**.'

I stepped forwards. 'I am **NOT**,' I said.

'Are too,' said Ralph.

'**Just wait until tomorrow**,' I said.

I knew what I had to do.

There was **only one way** to prove to Ralph, my class and the whole world that I wasn't **Scaredy-Cat Sam**.

After school that day, I went up to my room to put my plan in motion. It was a plan that required **extreme bravery**, but I was ready.

I was **NOT** going to be Scaredy-Cat Sam any more!

I went right up to Fang's tank. 'All right, Fang,' I said, staring him down. 'It's just **you and me.**'

'I'm here too, you know,' said Lucy. I didn't want to risk getting Fang out of his cage on my own, so Lucy was there **just in case** he decided to make another run for it. I reached in the tank, and picked him up the way the pet store owner had showed me. He wrapped **around my arm**. It was **terrifying.** But there were no incidents.

'I think he likes you!' said Lucy.

'I think he'd like to eat me,' I said, because I still wasn't totally sure that **Fang wouldn't eat me** if he had the chance.

I put him in the special travel container my parents had bought just for this very occasion.

'Make sure the lid is on!' said Lucy.

Butterbutt wandered in and started to attack my feet.

'Lucy! Get Butterbutt **out of here!**'

'Come on, Butterbutt,' she said.

I brought Fang's special container up

to my face so we were eye to eye. '**I'm counting on you**,' I said. 'And if you are going to eat anyone, make sure it's Ralph. <u>**NOT**</u> me, okay?'

Fang stuck his tongue out a couple of times.

I was pretty sure that meant **yes**.

CHAPTER 18

NOT AFRAID

'This is **my pet snake**. His name is Fang,' I said.

Ms Winkleworth had given me special permission to bring Fang to school and give a presentation on him.

'He likes to sit in his tank and **he eats mice**.'

'Does he bite?' someone asked.

I nodded. 'He's very **ferocious**. He just ate last night though, so we should be fine. But I wouldn't get **too close** if I were you. I'm a **snake-wrangler**, so I know what I'm doing.'

'**Wow**,' someone else said. It was Regina! 'Can I pet him?'

'I don't think we should **open his tank** in the classroom,' Ms Winkleworth said.

'I like snakes,' said Regina. She looked over her shoulder. 'But I think my brother is a little **scared** of them.'

Ralph was standing at the back of the classroom, as **far away from me** and Fang as possible.

'I'm **NOT** scared of that thing,' he said. 'I just don't like it, okay?' He didn't even snort, so I knew he must have been **scared**.

'Since you and Zoe and Bernard caught your snake and chased away your ghost, can you come over to our house?' said Regina. 'I bet you could get rid of **whatever is haunting our basement**.'

'What?' cried Zoe.

'Are you **crazy?**' said Bernard.

'**Absolutely**,' I said. I remembered what Spaceman Jack says whenever someone asks for his help. 'Whatever it is, I'm sure **we can handle it**.'

Because I'm **Sam Wu**. And I am <u>**NOT**</u> afraid.[10]

---

[10] I really, really, REALLY hope there isn't actually a zombie werewolf in their basement.

THE END

Katie and Kevin are definitely <u>NOT</u> afraid of answering some author questions

We all love Sam Wu! Is he based on one of you guys?

Katie: Between the two of us, I'd have to say Sam is more based on Kevin than me! I was more of a Lucy.

Kevin: I'll admit, I was a little bit of a scaredy-cat! But just like Sam, I always wanted to be brave. Some of Sam's adventures might even be based on my own childhood.

Have you ever done anything so scary that it made you want to pee your pants?

Katie: I'm <u>TERRIFIED</u> of heights, and one time on a hike with Kevin in China, I had to climb a 90 foot ladder! I was shaking the whole time, but luckily I didn't pee my pants.

Kevin: Unlike Sam, I <u>AM</u> afraid of sharks. I have never seen one in the wild, but if I did, I would probably pee my pants.

Spaceman Jack and Captain Jane from Space Blasters sound so cool! If you could be a famous TV show character, who would you be?

Katie: Sailor Moon from the *Sailor Moon* TV show! If you haven't seen it, it is a Japanese anime show about a girl named Serena who can turn into a superhero named Sailor Moon. She's been my favorite since I was seven and I still love her.

Kevin: My favorite is also from a Japanese anime show – Goku from *Dragon Ball Z*! He has the best super powers and isn't afraid of anything. Plus, like Sam Wu, he has awesome hair.

Sam eats some super tasty Chinese meals. What is the most delicious thing you have <u>EVER</u> eaten?

Katie: The most delicious thing I've ever had to eat is a type of spicy Chinese noodles called DanDan noodles. They are so spicy they make your mouth go numb – I love them! I also have a huge sweet tooth and love ice cream.

Kevin: My favorite thing to eat is sashimi – which is raw fish! I think Sam and Na-Na would be impressed.

Philip Zinkerman the Third is <u>NOT</u> our favourite person. Were you tempted to let him be chased by a ghost or eaten by a shark?

Even Ralph Philip Zinkerman doesn't deserve that !!!

And finally, what do you think is scariest . . . ghosts, sharks or the dark?

Katie: I'm <u>NOT</u> afraid of ghosts, sharks, or the dark.

Kevin: Sharks! Definitely sharks.

ACKNOWLEDGEMENTS

We love writing Sam Wu – but we couldn't have made it into a real book that you can hold in your hands without the help and support of some amazing people!

If we had our own space ship on Space Blasters, our captain would be Claire Wilson, our fearless agent who always guides us in the right direction. Thank you for believing in us and believing in Sam Wu.

We are tremendously grateful to everyone at Egmont for supporting Sam Wu! Thank you to our whole team of brilliant editors – Ali Dougal, Rachel Mann, Emily Sharratt, and Lindsey Heaven. We've loved working with all of you.

Huge thank you to our incredibly talented illustrator Nathan Reed for bringing Sam and his friends to life on the page! The illustrations are our favorite part of the book.

Thank you as well to genius designers Sam Perrett and Lizzie Gardiner who made the pages look so awesome, and to our publicist Siobhan McDermott, and everyone else at Egmont who worked on the book. We are so happy Sam Wu has found such a great home at Egmont.

We'd like to thank our families and friends for all their support and excitement. Special thank you to our grandparents: Mimi, Pop-Pop, Grandpa Bob, and Po-Po. And huge thanks and love to our siblings: Jack, Jane, and Stephanie.

And thank you to our parents, for everything.

Dive into Sam's next brilliant adventure!

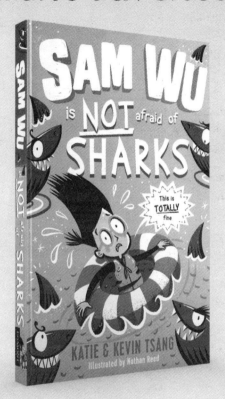

Sam Wu is definitely **NOT** afraid of the shark-infested waters when down at the beach with his friends. Nope, not at ALL.

You do **NOT** want to miss it!

No night light needed here because...

SAM WU

is <u>NOT</u> afraid of
THE DARK

EGMONT